# Gigi the Star

A.L. Geistkemper

*AuthorHouse*™
*1663 Liberty Drive*
*Bloomington, IN 47403*
*www.authorhouse.com*
*Phone: 1-800-839-8640*

*© 2009 A.L. Geistkemper. All rights reserved.*

*No part of this book may be reproduced, stored in a retrieval system, or transmitted by any means without the written permission of the author.*

*First published by AuthorHouse 12/21/2009*

*ISBN: 978-1-4490-1494-0 (e)*
*ISBN: 978-1-4490-1493-3 (sc)*

*Library of Congress Control Number: 2009913069*

*Printed in the United States of America*
*Bloomington, Indiana*

*This book is printed on acid-free paper.*

This book is dedicated to my Mom, Dad, sister Tiffany, BFF Karen, and my own dog Gigi.

Also thanks to God and Jesus


All of the dogs in this book are based on real dogs, except Coop and the dogs at the dog show. Skipper is based on my Dad's dog.

# Contents

The Dog Show .................................................. 1

Down The Chute ............................................. 5

Training .......................................................... 9

Almost Talent Night ..................................... 13

Now It's Talent Night .................................. 20

Gigi On The Road ......................................... 26

Skipper's Story ............................................... 32

Movie Magic .................................................. 38

Together Again .............................................. 43

Extra! Extra! Read All About it! ................ 49

# The Dog Show

"I've got you now!" barked Gigi, but before she could get to the squirrel, it ran up a tree. "Drat! That always happens!" the dog said. She walked back to the door to be let into the house. Gigi was a Shih Tzu. She was a small, white dog with a brown middle, and brown ears.

When Gigi got into the house, she jumped onto the top of the couch. That was her favorite place. She started to take a nap. Now, when you see dogs, they can be going for walks, or playing ball, or chasing their tail. All dogs do this. You think they are normal. You think they have no secrets. If you think this, you are WRONG. Dogs actually have a secret society. They make a hidden chute somewhere in their house and have a hidden button too. When they press the button it opens the chute, then the dog jumps in and slides down about twenty feet onto a cushion in a personal room. The room has toys, books, a calendar, a bed; anything a dog really wants.

The most important feature of the room is that it connects to a dog mailroom. There are twenty mailrooms per town so that it isn't crowded. Gigi's friends Riley and Niki delivered the mail. Riley was a Rottweiler and Niki was a Black Lab. Dogs got mail once or twice a month. The calendar marks the days that it is delivered.

Gigi woke up from her nap one hour later. It was time to pick up her owner's kids from school. Mom drove to Willow Elementary to pick up Miley and Carly. When they got there, four people were practicing for a golfing tournament. The balls they were hitting looked like small multi-colored tennis balls, and Gigi loved tennis balls. After Gigi was let of her leash in the schoolyard, she was so tempted by the balls that she darted of after each one. First a blue one, then a red one, next a green, then a yellow… it was so much fun! Everyone who saw her started laughing out loud.

Just then Miley came running, waving a piece of paper in her hand. "Mom! Mom! Look! Look! Look!" she said.

"What is it, honey?" asked Mom.

"There's a dog show next month! See?" Miley said, handing her the paper. "Can I enter Gigi?"

"Sure," said Mom. "But you'll have to train her!"

"Thanks, Mom! You're the best!" Miley said.

When Carly came they all went home. Gigi went to sleep very early, because the dog mail comes at night so no one will see it, and it was coming that night.

# Down The Chute

Gigi's secret chute was at the bottom of her toy basket, which was a good hiding place because she had so many toys. The button was hidden behind her Dad's pillow. Gigi had a high pitched alarm on her collar that only dogs could hear. She set the alarm for one o'clock A.M, and then she went to sleep on the bed. When the alarm woke her up, she turned it off and woke up Dad. Gigi took him to the door that led to the backyard like she did when she needed to go to the bathroom. When Dad got there she ran back to the room, jumped onto the bed, pressed the button, and lay on the pillow before Dad got back. Dad thought Gigi had just stolen his pillow because she wanted to sleep on it, so he pushed her aside and went to sleep.

Gigi snuck out of the room and went to her toy basket. Then she jumped! About five seconds later, she landed on the soft, pink pillow in her secret room. The room had a bookcase filled with books, a bed, a desk with paper and a pencil, along with some other things she needed. She also had some toys that had fallen into her room. Gigi went to the mail room. All of her friends were there waiting for the mail.

"Hi, Gigi!" they said. Now, Gigi had a lot of friends. Her friends in the mailroom were: Asia (the wise, brown dog who was Gigi's neighbor), Bailey (the poufy, white dog), George (the Fox Terrier who had a crush on Gigi and lived across the street), Gracie (George's sister who looked like him only smaller), Kobe (a small, gray dog who also had a crush on Gigi), Cassie (Kobe's sister who wore a shiny, pink bow because it was impossible to tell them apart), and Walter (a Yorkshire Terrier and had the biggest crush on Gigi).

"Mail call! Mail call!" yelped Riley as she and Niki came in with the mail. Dogs get a lot of mail so Riley and Niki pull carts with many mailboxes. Each mailbox holds mail inside for certain dogs. To open any mailbox's door, a dog has to put a paw on the scanner of his or her mailbox. The scanner identifies that dog by the paw print and lets in the correct dog. Gigi went to mailbox eight. She put her paw on the scanner and took her mail back to her room.

She got letters from Cassie, George, Kobe, and Walter, a new book called Royal Shih Tzus of China, and a Fashion Puppyz magazine. Gigi went out to show her friends the Fashion Puppyz magazine.

"Hey guys!" Gigi barked. "My owner Miley wants to enter me in dog show. Can you help me decide what to order for it?"

"Yeah, totally!" said Gracie. Gigi and the other nine dogs looked over the magazine for a few minutes.

"You should definitely get the gold collar," said Cassie.

"Don't forget to put a rose on it," said George.

"The red, satin ear bows will complete it!" exclaimed Bailey.

"Thanks for your help guys!" said Gigi. "Walter, can I borrow some dog treats to pay for the stuff?" Dogs don't have money so they use dog treats.

"Not at all," said Walter giving Gigi a googley-eyed stare. George and Kobe gave him a jealous look. They knew Gigi would ask Walter because he had more dog treats than any of them.

After Gigi had given her order and dog treat payment to Niki to deliver, Bailey said "Oh, before I forget, here's a little advice. At the dog show, remember to do the best that you can, because if there's a dog show, Princess will be there, and she'll do anything to win!"

# Training

"Who's Princess?" asked Gigi.

"She's Lauren's Chihuahua. Lauren is the most popular girl at Willow Elementary. She will do anything to win, and she is certain to enter the dog show," said Bailey.

"Then I better go back to bed!" said Gigi. "Press the ladder button, Riley!" Riley pressed a big, red button on the wall and ladders fell down the chute in each room. Gigi went up to her room and climbed up the ladder. She snuck back into her Mom and Dad's room, jumped onto the bed, and went to sleep. When Dad woke up and got out of bed to take a shower before work, Gigi stole his pillow and pressed the button behind his pillow to close the chute.

\* \* \* \* \*

Seven hours later Miley came into the room and said, "Let's start training for the dog show, Gigi". Miley and Gigi went onto their driveway. "Okay Gigi, let's start with the basics," said Miley. "Sit." Gigi sat. "Down," Gigi lay down. "Roll over," Gigi rolled over.

"Now let's work on agility," said Miley. She set up an obstacle course. There was a tire hung from a tree to jump through, an old see-saw to walk over, a line of plants on the side of the driveway to weave in and out of, rocks to jump over, and a stretch to the finish. "On your mark, get set, GO!" exclaimed Miley starting a stop watch. Gigi ran as fast as she could. She jumped through the tire, walked over the see-saw, weaved through the plants, jumped over the rocks, and sprinted to the finish. Miley stopped the stopwatch, and Gigi got a time of 12.14 seconds!

"That was a great time, Gigi!" said Miley. "Now let's work on style." Miley put Gigi in a pretty collar and matching ear bows. "We are going to practice walking down the runway. Remember to keep in step." They went down and back on the driveway almost flawlessly, but Miley tripped once. "That was amazing, Gigi!" said Miley. "Let's do this every day to get ready for the dog show. We are so going to beat Lauren Wik and her prissy Chihuahua Princess. Just wait!"

When they went inside the house, Gigi went into Mom and Dad's room. She made sure that no one was looking and pressed the chute button behind Dad's pillow. As it opened she slid down the chute and then pressed a button in her room to close it so the humans didn't find out about the dogs' secret society.

Gigi needed some quiet time after the big morning so she sat down on her bed with her hedgehog squeaky toy and started reading *Royal Shih Tzus of China*. It was about Shih Tzus that were given to kings and queens, lived in castles, had servants, and were treated like royalty. Gigi thought it was a good book. When she finished it, she pressed a button on her collar that called all of the other dogs to the mailroom. In a few minutes the other dogs had arrived. "What's up?" asked Kobe.

"Miley worked with me today for the dog show, and she is certain that I'm going to win!" said Gigi.

"I'm not so sure about the winning part," said Asia. "I was on a walk and my owner and I took a break. I saw Lauren and Princess training. Princess made the basics look like a piece of cake, and not the chocolate kind. Her agility time was astoundingly fast, and her style was indescribable!"

"But I still have a month," said Gigi confidently. "I can do this!"

# Almost Talent Night

The next few weeks of training went by so fast that Gigi was surprised when the night before the Willow Elementary Dog Show came. The dog mail was coming tonight and Gigi was supposed to get her brand new gold collar that she would put roses on and her new, red, shiny ear bows. Gigi set her collar alarm for one o'clock in the morning and went to sleep on her parent's bed right after she had dinner.

When her silent alarm went off at one A.M., she tricked her Dad into thinking she had to go to the bathroom again. She woke him up and took him to the door that led to the backyard. When he got there she ran back to the bedroom, jumped onto the bed, hit the button behind her Dad's pillow, and lounged on his pillow like she stole it until Dad got back.

When he got back to the bed, he pushed Gigi aside like usual and went to bed.

Gigi went to her secret toy basket chute and leaped in. Five seconds later she landed on her pink, fluffy pillow. She went out to the mailroom where Cassie, Kobe, Walter, Asia, Bailey, George, and Gracie were waiting.

"What's up?" asked Gracie waving to Gigi.

"Not much, except for the dog show," said Gigi.

"Mail call! Mail call!" exclaimed Niki as she and Riley came in with the mail carts. After they set up the carts, Gigi placed her paw on the scanner and got her mail. She took it back to her room to see what she got. She received a rose and a treat from Kobe, a Nature Beauty magazine, two roses and a treat from George, five roses and three treats from Walter, and her Fashion Puppyz magazine order package.

"Oh no!" shouted Gigi. All the dogs rushed into Gigi's room.

"What's wrong?" they said as they rushed in.

"Fashion Puppyz mixed up my order. They gave me a red, satin collar and gold ear bows," Gigi sighed.

Kobe said, "I have some sparkly, gold paint from a project you could use to paint the collar."

"And I have some shiny, red ear bows you could borrow," said Gracie.

"Could I use them?" asked Gigi.

"Sure," said Kobe and Gracie together.

"Thank you so much!" exclaimed Gigi.

George and Walter were jealous of Kobe because he was getting a lot of attention from Gigi and they liked Gigi too. Gracie went to get the bows and Kobe went to get the paint while Gigi picked out a collar that was in her room. Kobe came back with the paint and two small paintbrushes. They dipped the brushes in the paint and started painting the collar that Gigi picked out. When they were done, Gigi put the roses she was given onto the collar. Then Gracie came back with the ear bows.

"You can have the gold ear bows and satin collar," Gigi said to Gracie. "Thanks!" said Gracie. She put the accessories on. Then she gave Gigi the ear bows.

"Oh, and Gigi," said Niki. "We have a surprise for you. Come to the mailroom at six o'clock tomorrow."

"Okay!" said Gigi. "I can't wait to see what it is." She turned toward her room. "I have to go now. See ya!" said Gigi.

"Good-bye!" everyone yapped. Riley hit the ladder button. Gigi climbed up her chute, snuck into her parent's room, and fell asleep on the bed.

When her Dad got up to go to work, Gigi stole his pillow and pressed her chute button. After she had breakfast, Gigi set her silent collar alarm for six o'clock P.M. and slept the rest of the day.

When she woke up to her alarm, no one was home. The family was at the mall getting ready for the dog show. The show started at eight o'clock, so they had plenty of time. Gigi pressed the button behind her Dad's pillow and raced to her chute. She jumped down, landed on her soft, pink pillow, and sprinted to the mailroom.

All of her friends were there. "What's the surprise?" Gigi panted excitedly. "We are going to give you a makeover!" shouted Cassie and Gracie.

"No way!" yelped Gigi happily.

"Yep, first we'll start with a bath," said Niki. "I got a tub in the dog mail yesterday." Niki got out the tub and filled it with water that she had heated on the stove. Gigi got in the tub and Kobe started shampooing and rinsing her fur.

"Thanks," Gigi said to Kobe. "This is so nice."

George and Walter got jealous that Kobe was getting so much attention from Gigi. When the bath was done Walter blew Gigi's fur dry. Then Cassie brushed it and Gracie did her nails while George, Riley, and Asia held one mirror each so Gigi could see what was going on. Next, Bailey put the gold-painted collar and shiny, red ear bows on Gigi.

"And for the final touch," said Asia, "Perfume!" She put sweet smelling perfume on Gigi.

"Now with this look I'm sure to win first prize!" Gigi said excitedly. "Thank you so much everybody!" She gave everybody a hug. Walter, Kobe and George loved it the most.

Riley hit the ladder button and everyone went home. Gigi pressed the button in her parent's bedroom that closed the chute and waited for the family to come home so she could go to the dog show and be the champion.

A.L. Geistkemper

GIGI THE STAR

Gigi

v.s.

Princess

1 Night Only!

# Now Its Talent Night

When the family came home, the first thing they noticed was Gigi's new look. "Where did you get all of this stuff, Gigi?" asked Miley astounded. "Never mind. With this stuff we are so going to win! Let's go!" The family got on good clothes, got into the car and left for the dog show with Gigi. The show was at Mello Park.

When the family got there they saw everything. There was a catwalk for the style portion, places for the judges to look over the dogs, and an agility course. The basic tricks would be done when the judges looked over the dogs. Miley took Gigi to the place she would be looked over by the judges. Carly, Mom, and Dad sat in the chairs in front of the catwalk.

The first judge came over to Miley and Gigi. He was a man with brown hair and a beard. He was about thirty-five years-old, had blue eyes, and was wearing a dark blue tuxedo. He smiled and started taking notes about Gigi. He felt her to check her fur coat and to make sure she wasn't overweight. "Sit," he said. Gigi sat. "Down," he said. Gigi lay down. "Roll over," he said. Gigi rolled over. The judge wrote down the final score. "Good work," he said. The judge walked to the next place.

"Good work won't let you win," said a voice. Miley turned around and saw Lauren Wix.

"Oh it's you," said Miley. "Just back off."

"No, you back off," said Lauren. "Princess and I are going win... like always!" She began to cackle and cuddle her Chihuahua.

The next judge came to Miley and Gigi. She was an eighteen year-old woman with long, black hair and she was wearing a silky, red dress with matching high heels. She looked Gigi over like the first judge and took notes. She said the basic commands and Gigi did them when she said them. She wrote down Gigi's final score. "Very impressive work!" she said and moved on to the next table.

The last judge came. She was a forty-two year-old woman with short, red hair and she wore a silver, sequence dress. She checked Gigi and made her do the basic tricks. She wrote down the final score. "Your dog is amazing!" she said.

After the judges were done with all the dogs, the host, a twenty year-old man with black hair and green eyes who was wearing a dark green tuxedo, walked onto the stage and said "Hello! Welcome to the dog show! I'm the host, Matt Losery". The crowd clapped." It's time to get started with the finalists. After the judges are done judging they will give the four highest scores. The dogs with these scores will go on to the final round and compete for the aluminum, bronze, silver, and gold medals!" said the host. "And the four dogs are…" He took an envelope out of his pocket and opened it. He read the names of the top four scoring dogs. "Princess, London, Snickers, and Gigi! Would the dogs and their owners please come up onto the stage?" he announced. There was a lot of clapping.

The duos went up onto the catwalk stage. "Go behind the curtain, and when I announce your name, you'll walk down and back on the catwalk. Got it?" said Matt in a whisper. The owners nodded their heads and went behind the curtains. Matt went up to the microphone. "It's time for the style portion!" he said. There was a large amount of clapping.

"First is Mary Karo and her pooch, London!" he said. Mary and her grey Schnauzer walked down and back on the runway. They looked like they had practiced a lot. The judges were watching carefully and wrote down their scores.

"Next is Sara and her doggie, Snickers!" said the host. Sara and her multi-colored Yorkie strutted down the runway and back again in an impressive way. The judges wrote down their scores slower than they did for Mary, but still fairly quickly.

"Now it's Miley and Gigi's turn!" Matt said.

"Let's do this!" said Miley. They went out and marched down and back on the runway. Miley and Gigi were flawless and the judges were extremely impressed so they wrote their scores quickly.

"You were awesome, Gigi!" said Miley when she and Gigi finished walking.

"Last but not least, Lauren and Princess!" he said.

"Why does she get the better entrance?" Gigi thought. Lauren and her Chihuahua went down and back on the catwalk. They did a mixture of marching and strutting as they moved, but did a pose at the end which was sure to get them a higher score. The judges wrote down her score as soon as she finished.

"Now for the agility portion," said Matt. The course was like Gigi's, but bigger. There were four hoops to jump through, a see-saw to walk over, poles to weave in out of, a few hurdles to jump over, and a sprint to the finish.

"First up is Mary and London!" said the host. The dog went to the starting line and left after the whistle blew. She sprinted through all of the obstacles and had a time of 30.78 seconds.

"Now it's Sara and Snickers turn!" said Matt. The puppy left when she heard the shrill whistle. Snickers was very swift and did well at the impediments. When she crossed the finish line her time was 35.62.

"Next up is Miley and Gigi!" he said.

"Good luck!" Miley said to Gigi. Gigi went to the starting line. The whistle blew and Gigi was off like a rocket, through the hoops, up and down the see-saw, weaving through the poles, jumping over the hurdles, and sprinting to the finish. Gigi crossed the finish line and her time was 27.61 seconds.

"Awesome, Gigi!" Miley congratulated her.

"Princess will beat that," said Lauren.

"Lastly is Princess!" said the host. Princess stepped up to the starting line. The whistle blew and she shot off. She was so fast that everybody knew it was going to be a close time. Princess crossed the finish line. Her time was 27.62 seconds! One hundredth of a second slower than Gigi!

"Well, that's the end folks," said the host after everybody was back in their seats and the four finalists were on stage. "And the winner of Willow Elementary's 10th Annual Dog Show is…" He opened an envelope given to him from the eighteen year-old judge and read the winner. "Princess!"

# Gigi On The Road

Everyone was flabbergasted. "Second place goes to Gigi, third place goes to London, and fourth place goes to Snickers," the host said. The dogs lined up according to their placement.

"The aluminum medal and ten dollars go to Sara and Snickers!" the host said. The crowd clapped and Sara received the money and put the medal on her pup.

"The bronze medal and twenty dollars go to Mary and London!" he said. The clapping started again when Mary got the money and London got the medal.

"The silver medal and thirty dollars go to Miley and Gigi!" said Matt. There was thunderous clapping when Miley took the money graciously and Gigi wore the medal. "I got second place," thought Gigi sadly. "I'm not good enough for Miley."

"And the gold medal and fifty dollars goes to Lauren and Princess!" Matt exclaimed. There was quite a lot of clapping when the duo received their prize, but not as much as for Gigi and Miley. "Congratulations to all of the winners and have a good night!" said Matt Losery walking off the stage. The family went home a little disappointed but happy that Gigi got second place. When they reached their house, they got ready for bed, turned out the lights, and fell fast asleep.

Gigi was the only one awake that night. She couldn't fall asleep. She kept thinking about the dog show. "Miley really thought I was going to win, and I failed her," thought Gigi. "I can't bear to stay here anymore. My mind is made up. Tomorrow, I'm running away."

The next morning, before anyone was awake, Gigi got out her backpack that she had kept under her bed and filled it with meat and bottled water. Next she had to get out of the house. The burglar alarm was on and Gigi knew the combination to the system was 44444. She jumped onto a chair and pressed the number four five times. The alarm was off, so Gigi unlocked the door and managed to open it just enough to escape. "Now I won't be around for anybody to torment me about last night," thought Gigi. She started walking down the driveway. "Oh, I better take my collar of," she said. "So no one will know I belong to a family and try to take me back to the house." She unbuckled her collar and left it in the grass.

Gigi turned onto the street at the end of the driveway and saw a squirrel. Gigi had a thing for chasing them. "I'm going to get you!" Gigi barked at it. The squirrel shrieked and started to run toward the end of the block. "Oh no, you don't!" Gigi said running after the squirrel. She chased it to the end of the street and for the next ten blocks. Then the squirrel jumped onto the top of a car. Gigi jumped onto the hood of it, then onto the top. The squirrel jumped off and Gigi was about to follow when the car jerked and began to move. "What's going on?" Gigi asked herself. The driver began driving and Gigi felt the wind in her fur and felt like she was flying. "I think I'll hang out here for a while," said Gigi.

\* \* \* \* \*

Back at home, Gigi's family was frantically looking for her. They checked every room in the house before they realized the back door was a little bit open. Miley ran outside with tears in her eyes. "Gigi must have run away because she got second place at the dog show," she sobbed. "Gigi, where are you?!"

Gigi's friends had figured it out too when they tried to call her for a meeting. "She probably ran away because of the dog show and took her collar off," said Asia.

"I hope she's okay!" exclaimed George, Kobe, and Walter.

Right then, Miley found Gigi's collar and burst into tears. "I hope Gigi's alright!" she cried.

* * * * *

Meanwhile, Gigi was still riding mile after mile and saw everything from on top of the car. She mainly saw brick houses, cars, trees, and flowers, but she also saw a few other dogs, strange stone statues, a lake with ducks, and a fountain in a park. The thing she saw that most interested her was the city in the distance. As she went by, all of the people that saw her stared. Who wouldn't stare at a little dog, wearing a backpack, riding on the top of a big car?

The car finally stopped an hour later at a busy part of the city that Gigi had seen. She jumped off and found a nice, dark, quiet alley to eat some meat and drink some water. She sat in a corner of the alley and had her dinner. When Gigi had finished, she went to sleep because her big day had worn her out.

Gigi woke up early in the morning. It was raining and another dog was licking her face. "Who are you?" she asked the dog.

"First, let's go to a dry area," he said. "I have a cardboard box over there in the other corner of this alley." They moved into the box. "I'm Skipper," said a small black and white mutt. "I'm what most creatures would call a 'stray', but I prefer the term 'independent dog'. Who are you?"

"I'm Gigi," said Gigi. "I'm not an 'independent dog'. I had an owner, but I ran away because I let her down." She noticed that Skipper looked scrawny. "You look hungry," Gigi said. "Let me get my backpack." Gigi ran into the rain and got her turquoise backpack. Then she returned to the cardboard box and gave Skipper some ham and bottled water. He ate and drank heartily.

# Gigi the Star

"Thank you, chosen one," Skipper said when he had finished his meal. "Chosen one? What do you mean?" Gigi asked.

"Let me tell you a story," Skipper answered mysteriously.

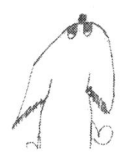

31

# Skippers Story

"Five years ago," Skipper started. "I lived with my mom, dad, two brothers, four sisters, and Grandpa. Grandpa was old and wise, so when I wasn't playing with my siblings, I was learning from him".

"He taught me how to listen to the trees and taste the air. He taught me how to see the invisible, how to smell fear and courage, and how to touch the magic in the world. But the most important lesson was about a dangerous force called Animal Control. They have a big, white van and tranquilizers and nets and... who knows what else? They can catch animals and take them away from our family, friends, and homes, that is, if they have any of those".

"Anyway, to survive in this city, we had to steal food from stores and restaurants. It all went well,

GIGI THE STAR

until one day someone called Animal Control and told them about our stealing. The big, white van came by our alley and spotted us. Everybody ran into a hiding spot. There weren't very many of them. I was able to hide under a trash can lid since I was the runt of the litter."

"What's that?" asked Gigi.

"The runt of the litter is the smallest of the puppies," said Skipper. "Really?" Gigi questioned.

"Well, that's what my brothers and sisters told me. I'm not sure if it's true or not. Let's get back to the story. Animal Control found everybody except for me. As they took my family away, my grandpa barked, "Skipper! You're our only hope! Find the chosen one! She'll give you food and water and she will be found in the rain!" Just as he finished, an Animal Control member put a muzzle on him and locked him in a cage. Then the van drove off with everybody in it except for me."

"I ate the food that we had stored until it ran out a year later. Then I ate the food I found on the ground in outside cafes and in trash cans because I didn't want to steal. That was why I was so skinny. Now you're here and you can help me get my family back!"

"Well, you're my friend now, and I have nothing else to do here, so I'll help you. Let's start now!" said Gigi.

"Okay, I made this plan for the day I met you," said Skipper, pulling out a piece of paper from a crack in his box. It had a bunch of words and designs on it.

"First we'll find the Animal Control Van. I wrote down the route on this piece of paper. When the driver stops at the Animal Control building, the manager will come out and help unpack the animals by bringing the cages into the building. The cages with animals are heavy because the workers usually put two or three animals into the same cage to avoid the cost of more cages. While they unpack, we will sneak into the building, get the keys, and set my family free!" Skipper explained.

"Shouldn't we free the other animals while we're there?" asked Gigi. "Yeah, I guess we should make it fair to the others." said Skipper.

"Let's start!" said Gigi and the dogs took off running.

"Turn right!" said Skipper. They turned right. "Take another right!" said Skipper. They turned right again. "Take a… WAIT!" yelled Skipper as he skidded to a stop. Gigi halted to a stop too, but not as fast as Skipper so she had to run back to him.

"What's wrong?" panted Gigi.

"I forgot to tell you the most important part of the mission," said Skipper. "Whatever you do, make sure the driver on the Animal Control Van doesn't see you or else he will think you are an 'independent dog' that steals food and he will capture you."

"Okay, I'll make sure he doesn't see me," said Gigi.

"Great, let's start again. Take a left," said Skipper. They took a left and ran straight for ten blocks.

"Okay, we stop here," said Skipper stopping at the corner of a street. Gigi stopped with him this time. "On the count of three, we jump out and run onto the edge of the Animal Control Van. Ready?" said Skipper.

"Oh, yeah!" said Gigi excitedly.

"Okay, 1…2…3!!!!" Skipper yelled and the dogs shot into the street, but something was wrong. There was a white van heading for them.

"A white van!" exclaimed Skipper. "Either my timing or my route map was off or maybe the Animal Control members changed the route, but it doesn't matter! The driver's seen us! Run!"

The dogs ran as fast as they could. The van followed them. Gigi and Skipper split up. Gigi took a left into an alley. Skipper took a right into the alley across from Gigi's. The van went into the left alley. Gigi hid in an overturned trash can. The bottom was facing toward the opening of the alley and it had a small hole so Gigi could look through it and see what was going on.

The van had parked in the opening of the alley. A man in a tuxedo stepped out of the van. "Wouldn't an Animal Control person wear something a little less fancy?" thought Gigi. The man had on dark sunglasses. He had red hair and a beard too. He started searching.

Gigi knew he was looking for her, but there was no escape. Even if she did get past the man, she couldn't get past the van which was so wide it could barely fit into the alley. For fifteen minutes the man looked for her. He checked each of the five trash cans and everywhere else Gigi could have hid. He gave up after checking Gigi's can and not finding her. He decided to go after the other dog and started toward the van. Suddenly, he turned around right before he got into the van and saw Gigi's eye in the peep hole of the trash can. He got a cage out of the van, ran toward the trash can, grabbed Gigi and swept her in the cage. Finally, the man threw Gigi into the back of the van and drove off with her.

# MOVIE MAGIC

Gigi was nervous. What would they do to her? When her eyes got used to the dark enclosure she saw where she was, but it didn't look like an Animal Control van. Gigi saw a few dim, twinkly lights, some fluffy, feathery boas, costumes of all kinds, and pictures of celebrities.

"Hey, what's up?" said a ten-year-old German Sheppard. "I'm Coop."

"What's going on? And why aren't you in a cage?" asked Gigi.

"I'm the director's dog. Why would I be in a cage? Oh, and you're going to be in a movie," he answered.

"What?!" Gigi exclaimed. "Isn't this Animal Control?"

"No way! Didn't you read the side of the van? It says Starlight Productions. You're going to be in a movie for the hottest Hollywood producers!" Coop explained.

Gigi was awestruck. Not only did Miley love movies by Starlight Productions, she saw every one of them one way or another. If Miley saw Gigi, she would come get her. "But, she probably won't notice me," Gigi thought, "so I'll just relax and live the celebrity life."

"By the way, what is your name?" asked Coop.

"Gigi," said Gigi.

"Okay Gigi, you're going to be in a movie called "Switched". Just do what the people tell you to do and you will be okay," he said. "They'll feed you, and you'll sleep in a comfy room."

"Okay, that's easy," said Gigi.

"But if you disobey you'll get no dinner and have to sleep in your cage," he said.

"Thanks for the advice," said Gigi. "Have some steak." She handed him some steak from her backpack.

"Thanks!" said Coop. He gobbled it down.

The van stopped at the studio. The man opened the trunk and took Gigi out. Coop jumped out. They entered the studio. Gigi saw bright lights, people in costumes and heard a lot of noise. She was taken to a certain set where she saw a man with a megaphone.

"That's my owner," said Coop who was following them.

Gigi's carrier went up to the director. "Sir, I've found a dog," said the man holding Gigi.

"Excellent! Now we can finish the movie!" said the director. He took Gigi out of her cage. "You play the queen's dog. In this scene you just lay down and eat this steak," he said giving Gigi a pep talk. He put Gigi on the bed with the steak. Gigi started eating. "And… action!" said the director as the camera people started filming. They filmed her for three seconds.

"Cut!" said the director. "Awesome, uh, we should give you a name. How about Mira? Awesome job Mira!"

"Mira? What kind of name is Mira?" thought Gigi. "Okay, next scene," the director said bringing Gigi to the next set. "Okay, when Darla walks into the room, stare at her for two seconds, and then run away." Coop's owner told Gigi on the way to another set. He got out of the way and yelled," Action!"

Darla came in. She started to say hi, but Gigi ran away.

"Cut!" he said. "Good job, Mira!" He moved Gigi to her last set. "Wait until Wendy comes in," he said putting her on the set floor. "When Wendy comes in, stare at her, then run right to her." He got out of the way of the camera and yelled "Action!"

Wendy came in. Gigi stared at her and then ran to her. Wendy took Gigi in her arms and they cuddled.

"Wow, I sure miss this," thought Gigi.

"Cut! That's a wrap!" yelled the director. "We finally finished! Let's have a party tomorrow for everybody who wants to come. We can announce the actors and actresses names and people can get their autographs!" Everyone who was working for the movie cheered. Then the director remembered Gigi.

"Jerry, take Mira to the Pet Apartment Dog Room for dinner and to rest up for tomorrow," he said. A tall, skinny man took Gigi. He went to a building across from the studio and went into a room with a bed, a meat buffet, water and a hot tub with a T.V. hanging above it.

Jerry left Gigi on the bed. He went back to the studio, shutting the door behind him. When he had gone, Gigi took off her backpack and put it beside the bed. Gigi ate dinner and then lounged in the hot tub with some water and watched a movie. When the movie was over, she went to bed, to dream about the big day she would have tomorrow.

# Together Again

The next day Gigi spent the whole day getting ready for the party. The staff washed her, brushed her and put a cute collar and matching ear bows on her. Gigi's nails were painted, too. She relaxed with a massage and some music. Gigi had a dinner of steak and baked Alaska.

When she finished her meal, a staff member named Mitchie took her to an amphitheater outside the studio. There was a huge crowd of people around it. Everyone in the county had shown up, including Miley and her family.

"Welcome to the movie preview party!" said the director stepping onto the stage. "My name is Duncan Shamen. I am the director of this film and this is my assistant, Courtney." He pointed to a woman off-stage. The crowd clapped.

"This movie is about a queen and a citizen who switch places for a day, but I won't tell you anymore. To start this off, I would like to introduce the actors and actresses of the new film "Switched".

"The first actress is Wendy Shawl, who plays the queen!" A woman with light brown hair and green eyes wearing a long, purple dress walked onto the stage. The crowd clapped.

"Next is Darla Shawl, Wendy's sister who plays the lucky citizen!" An identical woman wearing a pink dress walked onto the stage. The crowd clapped again.

Gigi was waiting for her turn to go onstage. Mitchie was holding her. Just then Gigi saw the white van belonging to Animal Control. "I promised Skipper I would help him get his family back, and that is what I'm going to do!" thought Gigi. She wriggled free of Mitchie's grasp and ran after the van.

"And that is Mira, the dog that plays the queen's pet!" Duncan said watching Gigi run past. The crowd clapped and cheered, thinking this was part of the act, but Miley yelled out, "That's Gigi! We have to go after her!"

Gigi caught up to the van and ran with it until it reached the Animal Control building. Gigi hid behind the trash next to the building's door. The manager came out to help unload the cages. Gigi snuck into the building and got the cage keys that were on the table by jumping onto a chair and then onto the table. She quickly went to the room where they kept the cages. There were ten cages filled with animals. In the third cage there was a family of black and white mutts.

"Are you Skipper's family?" asked Gigi.

"Yes," said Skipper's Grandpa. "And you are the chosen one. Am I not correct?"

"Oh, I'm the chosen one," Gigi said unlocking the cage door. "Now you guys are free!" She looked at the other animals. "All of the other animals look so sad, I'll free them too," Gigi said. She opened the cages. Soon all of the animals were running out of the building. The driver and manager were so surprised that they dropped all of their cages with animals. The door locks broke and those animals escape, too.

Skipper had tried out his plan earlier, but went straight to the Animal Control building. He saw all of the animals escaping. The ones that stood out the most were a group of dogs that looked like him. "Guys, is it really you?" he asked excitedly.

"Skipper!" his family cried. They all started hugging each other.

"I wish I had a family to do that with," said Gigi.

"You'll get one soon," Grandpa said.

"GIGI!" someone yelled. Gigi turned and saw Miley and started to back up.

"No, Gigi!" Miley yelled. "I've missed you terribly. I don't care if you won second place. I want you to come home. Please!!!"

Gigi stared at her. "So if it doesn't matter to Miley," thought Gigi, "it shouldn't matter to me either!" Gigi ran as fast as she could to Miley who took Gigi in her arms.

"Never leave us again!" said Miley who was so happy that she was crying. "Let's go back to the party," she said so they went back to the amphitheater.

"Hey, give us back Mira!" said Duncan the director.

"What?" asked Miley.

"I said, give us back our dog," he said.

"This isn't your dog, she's mine," Miley yelled holding Gigi tighter.

"We found her, she belongs to us," Duncan said reaching for the dog.

"But we owned her first, we found her again, and now you don't need her!" Miley shot back.

"Well we, er, we, well," he stammered. "Fine. You win. You can keep her." he said. "Bye, Mira, have fun at your real home." He patted her on the head. "You can still stay for the rest of the party," he said.

"We will," Miley said.

For the rest of the night they ate, danced, and sang. Then they watched "Switched". Like the director had said, there was a queen and a citizen who switched places. They did this because the queen was told she couldn't live a day like a regular person. She and a woman who looked like her switched places and a lot of crazy things happened, but they switched back the next day and everything was fine.

Do you want to know Gigi's part? First, she ate a meat to prove to the queen that her dog was spoiled when she denied it. Next, Gigi ran away from Darla, the fake queen, knowing it wasn't her owner. Last, Gigi ran to Wendy, the real queen, because she knew it was her loving owner.

After the movie the whole family went home. As they rode, a magical thing happened . One by one every animal that had escaped the Animal Control building, including Skipper's family, each found an owner that would hold it and love it. This was the best day of Gigi's life.

A.L. Geistkemper

# Extra! Extra! Read All About It!

"Good morning, Mom! Good morning, Dad! Good morning, Carly!" said Miley the next day.

"Good morning, Miley!" said everyone.

Dad was reading the newspaper, Mom was making bacon and eggs, and Carly was eating an apple. Gigi was the only one who had already finished breakfast.

"Gigi! How's my favorite dog ever?" asked Miley. She cuddled Gigi until breakfast was ready.

"Hey Miley, look at this!" said Dad handing her the paper. The headlines were: "Local Dog is Star and Hero", and the story under it read:

*A local dog named Gigi was seen at the Animal Control building minutes before the Great Animal Escape (see more on pg. 23) according to van driver, Tom Bobkin, who saw her go inside. He told the police about the Great Animal Escape and they think that Gigi must have gotten the keys to the cages and let the animals out. The police would have taken her to the pound, but Tom told them about Gigi's family who took her back, so they rejected the idea. Animal Control has decided to keep the animals in a big open area outside the building because of Gigi's heroic act. Gigi also appeared as the queen's dog in the new movie "Switched". She was at the big ceremony right before she chased Animal Control's van and freed the pets. The director of the movie, Duncan Shamen, loves dogs and adopted a family of black and white mutts to keep his own dog, Coop, company. For now, Gigi is an ordinary house dog with the most extraordinary story a dog has ever had.*

When Miley finished reading she flipped through the pages looking for the comics, but something caught her eye. "Hey guys, look at this!" yelled Miley. The family crowded around the paper. "It's the results of the dog show. It says that one of the judges confessed that Lauren Wix had bribed them so she could win. That means Gigi really got first place! We can go to the school tomorrow and exchange the medals and get our prize money," she said.

The whole family was thrilled. Gigi heard it too. She couldn't wait to tell her friends. When the family went to the mall, Gigi opened her chute and went down to her secret room. She put away her backpack and then called her friends with the button on her collar that Miley had put back on. Her friends came down and saw her.

"Gigi!!!" they barked and ran to hug her. "Our owners read us the newspaper story about you" said Cassie.

"I'm so glad you're back," said Walter to Gigi.

"That's not even the best part!" said Gigi. "The newspaper article had the results of the dog show and Lauren Wix bribed the judges, so I get the gold medal!"

"That's awesome!" shouted the other dogs.

"I'm going to get it tomorrow," she said. "I hope you'll be there!"

"We'll be there," said Asia.

"But for now have some meat!" said Gigi giving them what was left over from her backpack.

\* \* \* \* \*

The next day at 7:00 P.M. Gigi went, all dressed-up, to the school auditorium. Miley turned in the silver medal. She then lined up with Mary and Sara. Lauren came in and reluctantly turned in her gold medal and forty dollars of the winner's money. She lined up with the rest of the girls.

"All right, let's get down to business!" said Matt the host. The crowd was getting anxious. "The real results are in, and the aluminum medal goes to Lauren and Princess!" said Mr. Losery. There was polite clapping as Lauren took the medal with a pout.

"The bronze medal and ten more dollars go to Sara and Snickers!" said the host. The crowd clapped more as the owner received ten more dollars and the dog got the prize.

"The silver medal and ten more dollars go to Mary and London!" he said. There was a lot of clapping as the team received the medal and money.

"And the gold medal and twenty more dollars go to Willow Elementary's first ever dog show winner… Miley and Gigi!!!" Matt exclaimed. There was thunderous clapping and cheering as Miley got the money and Gigi got the medal.

# Gigi the Star

As it was placed on her, Gigi felt like she was on top of the world. Best of all, she saw all of her friends and their owners as well as Miley and her family among the crowd full of students and fans. She knew this was where she belonged. She had pleased her owner, but most of all, she had pleased herself. She knew that the real winner was inside of her.

Gigi the hero and Gigi the star!!

A.L. GEISTKEMPER

All of the dogs in this book are real except Coop and the dogs at the dog show. Skipper was based on my dad's dog.

# About The Author

A.L. Geistkemper is 11 years old and lives in Texas with her family and her dog Gigi. Gigi was the inspiration for this book. She also lives with her sister's guinea pigs, which she dislikes A LOT. This is her first publication.